SCOUNDRELS OF THE COURT:
LADY MARGERY'S LOVER

A HISTORICAL ROMANCE SERIES

BY MARY SCOTT

Scoundrels of The Court: Lady Margery's Lover

COMING SOON FROM MARY SCOTT!

STAY IN TOUCH WITH MARY SCOTT!

For FREE sneak peek content, please sign up for our newsletter:

www.maryscottbooks.com

CONTENTS

CHAPTER 1

On a mild summer's day, Margery (Meg) Parnell felt a rush of water between her legs. She would have investigated it, but she could see nothing beyond her large belly. "Mavis!" she bellowed. "It is time!"

A portly servant rushed to her lady's aid. "Linens! Hot water!" the servant barked at another member of staff for the manor. Meg Parnell was lead to a birthing chair that had been placed in front of the fire in her bedchamber. Linens and a pitcher of freshly boiled water lay on a table ne

xt to the birthing chair, along with a jug of wine and ale for whatever preference the lady would have at the time.

Meg clutched her stomach as another contraction coursed through her body. She groaned through the pain while making her way to the birthing chair with Mavis' help. Mavis helped her shed her clothing until she had nothing but her chemise on, to help make the birth easier. When Meg was placed in the chair, resting in between contractions, Mavis sent for the husband of Meg, James Parnell. After a time, he had not arrived.

"Where is he?" Meg cried through her pain.

Mavis wet Meg's lips with wine to maintain her energy. "I know not, Madame. I sent for him a long while ago now. I shall send for him agai-" she was interrupted by another servant that has rushed in.

"Master Parnell wishes to not be involved in the matter," the servant told Mavis after curtseying.

"Dastard!" Meg wailed.

"Breathe, Madame. Please breathe. It will be over quickly. You have the hips of a mother," Mavis tried to calm down her mistress.

"I will never have another child again!" Meg wailed again. She gripped the arms of the chair so hard, all of her fingers whitened. "This dastard better be a son!"

"Aye, Madame! This will be a son for you and Master. Now, push!" Mavis instructed Meg to start pushing to introduce the new heir to the world.

"Ahhh!" Meg cried. She tried again, and again, to push as hard as she could. She wanted desperately for this to be over.

"Come! One more and the bairn is here!" Mavis encouraged.

One final cry from Meg, and then a smaller cry was heard in the room. Meg collapsed in the chair after hours of labor, and Mavis severed the cord and cleaned the newly birthed Parnell. She cleaned the mess from the child's lips and heard someone open the door to the bedchamber. Behind her, James Parnell entered the room. He made his way to Mavis, looked at the child, and only said one thing:

"A son?"

Mavis had not even tried to sex the child, for how involved she was in the care of it. She opened the linen she had swaddled the child in, peered at what she needed to, and looked up at James Parnell from her kneeling position. "A girl," she stated.

James' face betrayed no emotion. He simply nodded and left the room. Mavis looked back at the new little life in her arms, and smiled. She inherited her mother's beautiful copper hair, and it would be seen what her little eyes would look like. She bounced the little thing in her arms as she began to cry, which brought Meg out of her small rest.

"A boy?" she asked, her voice filled with optimism.

"A girl, Madame. But she is strong, healthy, and full of vigor. You will birth a son next time, I know it."

"God's bones!" Meg swore. "I cannot do this again, Mavis. I feel so ill! Please send for the servant Mary to tend to me. You may take the child and tend to her," Meg waved her away.

Mavis was slightly upset about how flippant Meg seemed. Even if the child was not a son, they had both survived the birth and the child was healthier than many that had been born before. "What of a name for her?" she asked Meg as she stood up to take the child away.

"I do not care."

Fine, Mavis thought. She let Meg remain in her chair as she took the child away to be properly bathed. What would she name the child? It seemed that Meg nor James would care. She gently poured warm water over the child's body to clean off what remained of the birth until only beautiful, pink skin remained. She admired all of her little fingers, toes, and all of the folds in her little body. What would be a perfect name for her?

"Is Madame Margery alright?" a voice asked. She glanced behind her to see the Lord of the manor, Alfred Parnell.

Mavis beamed at her Lord. "It is good to see you, my Lord." She turned around and offered the small bundle to Alfred. "Madame and child are both alive and well."

Alfred's eyes sparkled as he took the little girl into his arms. He gazed upon her in wonder, a smile across his entire face. "A boy? No, a girl. A boy would not be as beautiful as this little darling. Does she have a name?"

"Nay. Madame did not care for the child not being a son, and neither did Master James."

"Ah, then we must name this precious one!" Alfred said a little too loudly. The child began crying, making both Mavis and Alfred wince.

"She does wail like her mother, aye," Mavis said off-handedly.

"Mayhap she has her mother's spirit," Alfred mused.

"Spirit? It is a pestilence."

"Hush, Mavis. Meg herself is young and spoiled. She knows not of the world like you or I," Alfred chastised Mavis. "What about Margery? It is a beautiful name, for a beautiful child."

"She is eventually to be your heir, Lord. After your beloved wife and only child perished in childbirth. Rest their souls."

Alfred was sad for a second, but smiled when he had decided. "Aye. She shall be Margery Parnell II, and she will make the most beautiful little lady."

CHAPTER 2

Margery Parnell II was raised to be strong, intelligent, and compassionate. She excelled in her Latin and French tutelage, impressed her Uncle Alfred with her aptitude in piano, and rode her precious pony with skill beyond her years. James Parnell intended for his daughter to be a pawn in a beneficial marriage, and his other brother, Richard, just enjoyed a leisurely life at Highrell Manor. Alfred Parnell, Lord of Highrell, intended for Margery to inherit the lands after him. There were no more heirs in the family, and he had become a widower during the birth of what would have been his son. Little Margery would have all of what he had, that he was sure of. At the age of six, she still had that copper hair (with a fiery temperament), and she had inherited her father's blue eyes. She would break hearts one day, and she would find a husband that would be an asset to her, and Highrell. James and Meg Parnell were mostly absent parents, and barely spoke to each other themselves. They never conceived again after their daughter, and divorce was not possible within their Catholic faith.

During the winter before Margery's seventh birthday, Alfred had begun planning a feast for the prominent people of Highrell. Invited to the event were merchants, businessmen, entrepreneurs, and other people of higher status. Alfred envisioned a prosperous Highrell with all of its elements working well together, and he needed to develop it. Margery could also learn alongside her uncle, while he strengthened what held Highrell together. While she was still young, her beloved Uncle could see that she would have a mind fit for financial strategy and arithmetic. She would be able to handle the running of Highrell when Alfred was gone and it was her time. Until then, she would learn these skills alongside her typical 'feminine' tutelage.

In preparation for that night's feast, a beautiful array of pies, platters and sweets were being prepared. Fresh fruits and grapes from the orchards were arranged on the tables, and barrels of deliciously sweet mead, wine, and ale were at the ready for the occasion. The cooks and servants were hard at work preparing the manor, and Margery's helpers were working harder.

"These sleeves itch!" little Margery screeched. "Ow!" she wailed. "Your pin struck me!"

"Hush!" Mavis admonished Margery. "Your mother would be very displeased with me, and you, if you were not ready for the banquet this evening."

"I do not want to be paraded around!" Margery protested. "I want to ride my pony with the stable boy, Peter."

"You may ride your beasties with him tomorrow, little miss. You may make new friends this eve! I am sure there are many other children for you to play with." Mavis continued to pin Margery's clothing in place.

She was dressed in the most beautiful blue dress that evening, bringing out her eyes. Mavis knew she'd break many hearts when she was of marrying age.

"There! All finished now," Mavis finished pinning Margery's hair back. "You may now *carefully* enjoy the party tonight, little Madame."

"Thank you Mavis," Margery said in her rehearsed, sing-song voice.

"Now run along."

Margery dutifully nodded her head. Mavis smiled when she noticed the little girl walking more carefully than she had before.

The event was in full swing. The dance hall of Highrell Manor was filled with people dancing gaily and eating heartily. Beautiful string music was playing, the women were dancing, and the men were talking. Stood in a quieter corner of the manor was Alfred and a man named Thomas Bennett. The man was a prosperous and business-savvy merchant with men under him in a carpentry business, with customers from all around England. He began as a simple carpenter himself and made smart investments until he was one of the wealthiest businessmen in all of Highrell. Even the King – Henry VIII – himself had purchased one of his credenzas. The men were discussing improving the output of Bennett's business when little Margery came trotting along.

"Uncle, I want a meat pie and there are none left on the table," her small voice demanded.

Alfred broke his conversation and looked down at his beloved niece. "Have you asked the cook if there are any remaining?"

Margery's face erupted in a look of realization. "Thank you, Uncle. I will ask of the cook if there are any left".

"Who was that?" a young boy asked as he approached Alfred and Master Bennett.

"Ah! Alfred, this is my boy, Thomas," Thomas Bennett II introduced his son, a young lad with brown hair and hazel eyes. He was quiet, but it was evident that he was paying attention to his surroundings.

"It is a pleasure to meet you, boy," Alfred shook his hand. "How old are you?"

Thomas Bennett III spoke up, "I am ten years old."

"What a fine age!" Alfred exaggerated. "You'll soon make a fine young man. The young miss you just saw was my niece, Margery."

"May I play with her?" the boy asked.

"If your father accepts, you may play with Margery for the rest of the evening. What do you say, Thomas?" Alfred asked Thomas (the senior).

"Aye, run along, boy. You must grow bored of this business chatter," Thomas (the senior) patted his son on the back and ushered him away. He looked at his progeny as he rushed off. "He'd be looking for a possible wife in a few years. I have been ill with an ague lately, and it has made me realize we need to ensure our family's future."

Alfred nodded in understanding. "Aye. My Margery is the closest thing to a progeny that I have. Despite her only being six years old, possible suitors need to be considered in a few years as well. A betrothal would be best."

The men continued to chat about these things that were trivial to their young progenies.

CHAPTER 3

"Hello," young Thomas Bennett greeted Margery.

Margery had snuck away into a corner to eat her meat pie.

"This is mine and I asked the cook for it," she stated.

"I just came to say hello."

"Oh… hello. Who are you?"

"My name is Thomas Bennett. My father was the gentleman conversing with your uncle in the hall."

Margery considered this for a moment. She reached into her pockets and withdrew some sugared pear drops. "Would you like a pear drop?" she offered Thomas.

"I thought you did not want to share?" Thomas asked Margery, seeming quite confused.

"I had not decided if I liked you yet. But I have decided that I like you, therefore, you may have one of my pear drops."

"Thank you," Thomas accepted. "Did you have to ask the cook for these?" he asked teasingly.

Margery snickered. "No. I took these from the main table. Please do not tell my uncle. I can snatch more for us later if you would like."

Thomas held his lips closed with his thumb and forefinger, showing Margery that his lips were sealed. Margery beamed at her new friend. "I am pleased to have met you tonight, Thomas."

Thomas agreed. The two spent the rest of the evening frolicking around Highrell Manor.

Over the next month, Thomas Bennett II and Alfred Parnell frequently met to discuss business while Margery and Thomas (the junior) played together around Highrell Manor and its gardens. They knew not of what the men in their lives were doing, but they enjoyed their games, archery, and horse riding. Thomas enjoyed a lesson or two with Margery while he visited the manor, as it was well known that Alfred hired the best tutors for his niece. While Margery was wilder and wished to be outside, Thomas was more of the perfect student. He was studious and he worked hard, but Margery seemed to have more natural talent for the languages and musical pursuits.

"Thomassss," Margery whined. "I want to ride my pony and play in the garden!"

Thomas stopped his piano playing abruptly, the aborted musical note hanging in the air. "I am busy, Margery." The piano tutor resumed his instruction.

"We shall not be friends if you deny me!"

"Then, we will not," Thomas said flippantly.

Margery pouted and her eyes filled with tears. "Surely, you jest?"

"Were you jesting?"

"…Yes," Margery begrudgingly admitted.

"Then why say that at all?"

"I just want to play with you! I have no brothers or sisters or cousins."

Thomas rolled his eyes. "Fine," he sighed. "Please, let me finish this song and then we can play any game you would like."

"Fine," Margery huffed. She watched Thomas play his song. He was only ten, but he was a lot older to her and she admired how his large hands were able to glide across the keys so smoothly, and how he was able to play so beautifully.

"That sounds pretty," she said, sitting next to him on the piano stool.

"You, too, could play like this. You are fortunate to have such an accomplished tutor. When you are my age, you will play melodies such as this."

"I do not want to only play music. I want to ride horses, practice archery, and all sorts of things people say are only for boys."

"There," Thomas finished.

Margery grabbed him by the arm again, and dragged him to the gardens of Highrell and to the stables. She told him she wished to ride her pony, and the stable hand assisted her and Thomas in preparing her pony and a horse for him. They rode their beasts the entire afternoon and had the most splendid time. They arrived back at the stables and Margery handed her pony off to the stable hand. She walked out of the stables, forgetting Thomas, then turned to find him removing his horse's saddle and bridle.

"Why are you doing that? The stable hand will do it," she asked Thomas.

"Father taught me how to look after the horses. And I like it, I feel terrible leaving all of my tasks to the servants sometimes."

Margery considered this for a moment. "Curious, but that's what they're for. So we can have fun!"

Thomas paused brushing his horse. "Have you considered that they do not have much fun themselves, when all they do is serve us?"

"No, but that is what our families hire them for."

"Many servants do not wish to be servants. They did not dream of cleaning up after us, Margery. They are doing what they must to survive. How rude are you to your own servants?"

Margery looked at her feet, suddenly embarrassed. "Maybe slightly, I know not," she traced shapes into the dirt with her foot, not willing to look at Thomas directly.

"Do you understand it now?" Thomas pressed her. "We live quite charmed and easy lives, with our biggest worries being our studies, and eventually, marriage and heirs one day. Our servants worry about sending enough money home to feed their families, and they may never marry and enjoy that part of life that we experience. I have not done this to admonish you, Margery. However, I hope you can consider your actions."

"I have never heard any other Lords or Ladies express such an opinion."

Thomas chuckled weakly, "My father is not a Lord. He is wealthy, and we live very comfortably, but he is not a lord."

"I hope you do not think less of me," Margery said to Thomas in the smallest voice he had ever heard from her.

"I do not," Thomas said in a comforting voice. "I am just passionate about the topic. My father's business dealings have made me realize that our world is a lot more cruel when you are not a noble."

"I will try to be as pleasant to our servants as possible, then," Margery decided.

"Would you like any help with the horse?" she asked Thomas.

"Actually, yes," Thomas replied. He picked up another horse brush and held it out for Margery to take. She accepted the brush, and sat down on the bench next to him. Beginning to brush the horse, Margery found the activity calming. She felt the slow repetition centering.

"I think we shall be great friends, Thomas Bennett," she said surely.

"Aye, I agree," Thomas said.

CHAPTER 4

"Uncle," Margery dragged. "I have had enough of the ledgers for today. I want to go outside and practice my archery."

Alfred chuckled at his niece. "Margery, just a few more entries. You need to understand how to manage the finances, oversee business, and many more things."

"My head hurts terribly. Please."

"Fine," Alfred sighed. "But we must resume tomorrow."

"Yes! Anything for me to just leave now!" Margery rushed off and left her uncle with Highrell's ledgers open.

Will that girl ever sit still? Alfred wondered to himself. She was still so young and filled with so much vigor, while he could feel the effects of age on his bones. He needed to instruct Margery on how to manage his lands, but the young lass' attention would wane. While this was frustrating, Alfred tried to remember what it was like being young. The realities of the world were so far away from him, and all he wanted was to explore. Alright, he would be patient during these tumultuous adolescent years. She was now fifteen, and starting to become a lady.

As Margery was now of marrying age, other Lords and other suitors had begun visiting the manor to enquire about courting and betrothal. While this was natural process, especially for women of Margery's somewhat higher status – Alfred did dread the idea of his daughter-figure fully growing up. He had, essentially, raised her; and he wished she was still that small little girl with the fiery red hair that cared for naught other than her toys and her playtime.

Thomas Bennett II and his son were due to arrive that day for a visit of leisure. This was a rare occurrence, as Alfred and Thomas had developed a close business relationship over the decade (roughly) that they had been friends. For the Bennetts to only visit for visiting's sake was quite the pleasure to Alfred… and Margery, of course. They were ready in the foyer of Highrell Manor to accept Thomas senior and junior. Margery was dressed in a dress of beautiful emerald green fabric with silver embroidery details and her hair was loose but pinned back in a style befitting of a young lady like her.

A carriage stopped in front of the main door of the manor and out climbed the two Bennett Men. Alfred watched as Margery blushed when she saw the younger Bennett man, which even he could understand. The boy had grown into a strapping young man at nineteen years old; he was tall and muscular, his hazel eyes were striking and his brown hair had natural highlights from the time he spent outside in the sun. Alfred giggled to himself after noting Margery's blushing as Thomas (the senior) stepped out of the carriage. He had become less of a vision, as he had become quite portly and his face seemed to be permanently red. However, he remained a good man with more joy in his personality than many men of his age. Margery rushed away with Thomas to ride their horses around the forests and grounds of Highrell Manor. Now left alone, Alfred and Thomas (the senior) entered the manor to begin their visit.

"Alfred! My dear friend," Thomas (the senior) embraced Alfred Parnell.

"It is good to see you," Alfred smiled, his eyes wrinkling at the corners.

Alfred beckoned a servant to bring the men a small platter of food and plenty of ale. They sat down in the music room and sunk into the plush settees that furnished the room. "What a comfortable place to rest my weary legs!" Alfred exclaimed, teasing his friend. "I wonder *who* could have engineered such a fine seat!"

Thomas (the senior) smiled and waved dismissively. "These are not made by my hands anymore, Alfred."

"Ah, but you did hire magnificent carpenters and apprentices to continue creating to your standards," Alfred sipped his ale and nibbled on some bread and cheese.

"You have always been too kind, friend," Thomas' large fingers fed some sweet almond paste into his mouth. "Alfred, I have something to ask of you."

Alfred glanced at Thomas. "Of course, my friend," he tried not to say hesitantly. He trusted Thomas, but he seemed to be broaching the subject somewhat suspiciously.

"How old is your niece now?"

"She has just turned fifteen, why do you ask?"

"My son is now well within the correct age to marry, and I must consider the future of his inheritance and heirs. He and Margery have been quite… close, for some time now, yes?"

Knowing where this was going, Alfred decided to act ignorant until Thomas came out with it. "Yes, I believe so. Almost ten years. They befriended each other the same night we did: at the banquet I hosted."

Thomas nodded, seeming quite serious. "I do not ask this purely for the benefit of status and breeding. However, it would not *not* be beneficial if you were to accept this, as we are friends as well and I think this would be an ideal match.

"Alfred, what say you about marriage between my Thomas and your Margery?"

Feigning consideration, Alfred acted pensive for a few moments. Thomas fidgeted in that time, seeming quite nervous. "Why, Thomas," Alfred beamed. "I thought that was the plan all along. We shall arrange the betrothal and announce it formally. Our two progenies shall be united in matrimony."

CHAPTER 5

Margery and Thomas were now in the forests of Highrell, their favorite space to sneak away to. Thomas let himself rest against the tree, opening his arms to accept Margery. His hands gestured a beckoning motion, and she accepted his offer. She knelt down and settled herself in his arms until she was encircled in his embrace and leaning against him while he was leaning against the tree. He stroked her hair tenderly and absentmindedly kissed her head.

"I love that," Margery sighed. She closed her eyes and enjoyed this moment of quiet bliss.

"And *I* love you," Thomas said, to which, Margery lifted her head and accepted a kiss from him.

"Most blessed of birthdays to you, my love," Thomas whispered, planting another soft kiss on Margery's lips.

The two lovers settled in each other's loving embrace and watched the world go by from under their tree. The grass around them swayed from a gentle breeze that was also cooling and peaceful. Small cracklings could be heard around them from small insects and they even noted a small hare hopping into their field of view. They both glanced at it for a moment, but they turned their attentions back to each other. They did not hear anything else besides the breeze, forest, and their own breathing.

Thomas' voice broke the silence. "What present would you like for your blessed day?"

Margery feigned her consideration of the topic for a moment and attempted to seem pensive. She tutted after a few seconds, seeming to then know exactly what she wanted. Her gaze turned to Thomas, a coy smile on her lips. "Kiss me, then I will tell you". A small kiss was placed on her lips. Thomas withdrew and looked amused, and slightly confused.

Margery thanked him. "Now, all I have wanted for every blessed day since I was six years old… is you." She stated this demurely, not wanting to seem wanton in her pursuits. She played with the hair as the nape of his neck.

Thomas' hazel eyes narrowed in confusion for a moment, before he seemed to realize what Margery wanted, a twinkle in his eye. "Aye, are you sure?" he asked of Margery, making sure they both were in agreement. Margery nodded, and kissed Thomas with a fervor he had never felt before.

Margery grabbed Thomas' hair at the nape of his neck and drew his body to hers as close as humanly possible. Her other hand caressed his cheek, and he rested his own against hers. Every moment passing was just filled with them trying to be as close as possible. Margery thought herself quite bold; her tongue seeking out his when their lips parted. As their kiss deepened, she felt Thomas' large hand on her breast.

Margery moaned. "*Oh*, Thomas. Please make me a woman this day," she murmured into their kiss.

Thomas embraced Margery and used his hold on her to shift their position until she had been placed gently on her back on the grass. She watched as his eyes poured over her body hungrily. His hands followed, feeling every bit of her as he kissed her. Now on top of her, his grasp went to her breasts, hips, bottom, thighs, and every other bit of curve he could feel. Margery's curvy body was sought after of noble women at the time, showing her wealth and ability to feast on rich and delicious food.

"*Ugh*," Thomas grunted. "I love how you feel," he said gruffly. His tone was heavy with desire.

Margery rushed to help him lift her skirts; both of them impatient to get to the point. Thomas' hands gripped Margery's hips as he positioned himself between them.

"Please, I need to be with you," Margery begged. She tried to loosen his clothing to let his body free.

Thomas kissed her neck and nipped the skin gently with his teeth. Margery hoped in a fleeting moment that he had not left a bruise, but she stopped caring when his lips were placed on her collar bone and trailed down her sternum. She moaned as he removed her brocade, skirts, and chemise until she was completely bare. She felt a small chill in the air, but her body was warmed by his own bare chest as he rested on top of her, having removed his own shirt as well. They just kissed for that moment until they both were breathless.

Margery's blue eyes met Thomas' hazel ones, and in those beautiful brown-green irises she knew that she was with the love of her life. "I love you," she breathed.

"And I you," Thomas repeated. He removed his breeches and readied himself, before Margery seemed to panic.

"What is wrong?" Thomas asked. He immediately ceased.

"What if God can see us?" Margery asked nervously.

"He can," Thomas chuckled. "But I am certain he will understand. We plan to marry regardless."

Margery covered herself and glanced around her cautiously. "What if someone else can see us?"

Thomas caressed her body gently. While Margery was worried he would be upset, his gaze still seemed to be loving.

"What is truly worrying you, dear?"

Margery glanced away from Thomas and tried to collect her thoughts. "What... what if we regret not waiting until we are wed?"

Thomas covered Margery with her skirts after she had begun shivering. "I know I would not regret it," he said. Margery's heart sank. Would he now erase their relationship if she did not want to continue?

"But if you would, we need not continue today," Thomas stated.

Surprised, Margery did not know what to say. "I must admit, I did not think you'd be so understanding". She was kissed by Thomas, who withdrew and looked at her with an intense, loving gaze.

"I love you. It matters not when we act as husband and wife, as long as you would always have me as a husband. We have the rest of our lives for sex. I am content with just loving you," Thomas said, then a wicked smile formed on his lips. "But I would enjoy this kissing and fondling until then."

The lovers continued to cuddle the afternoon away until they had to redress themselves and part ways for the day…

THE STORY CONTINUES WITH SCOUNDRELS
OF THE COURT: LADY MARGERY'S SACRIFICE

Get it HERE: www.mybook.to/ladysacrifice

COMING SOON FROM MARY SCOTT!

STAY IN TOUCH WITH MARY SCOTT!

For FREE sneak peek content, please sign up for our newsletter:

www.maryscottbooks.com

9 798684 483615